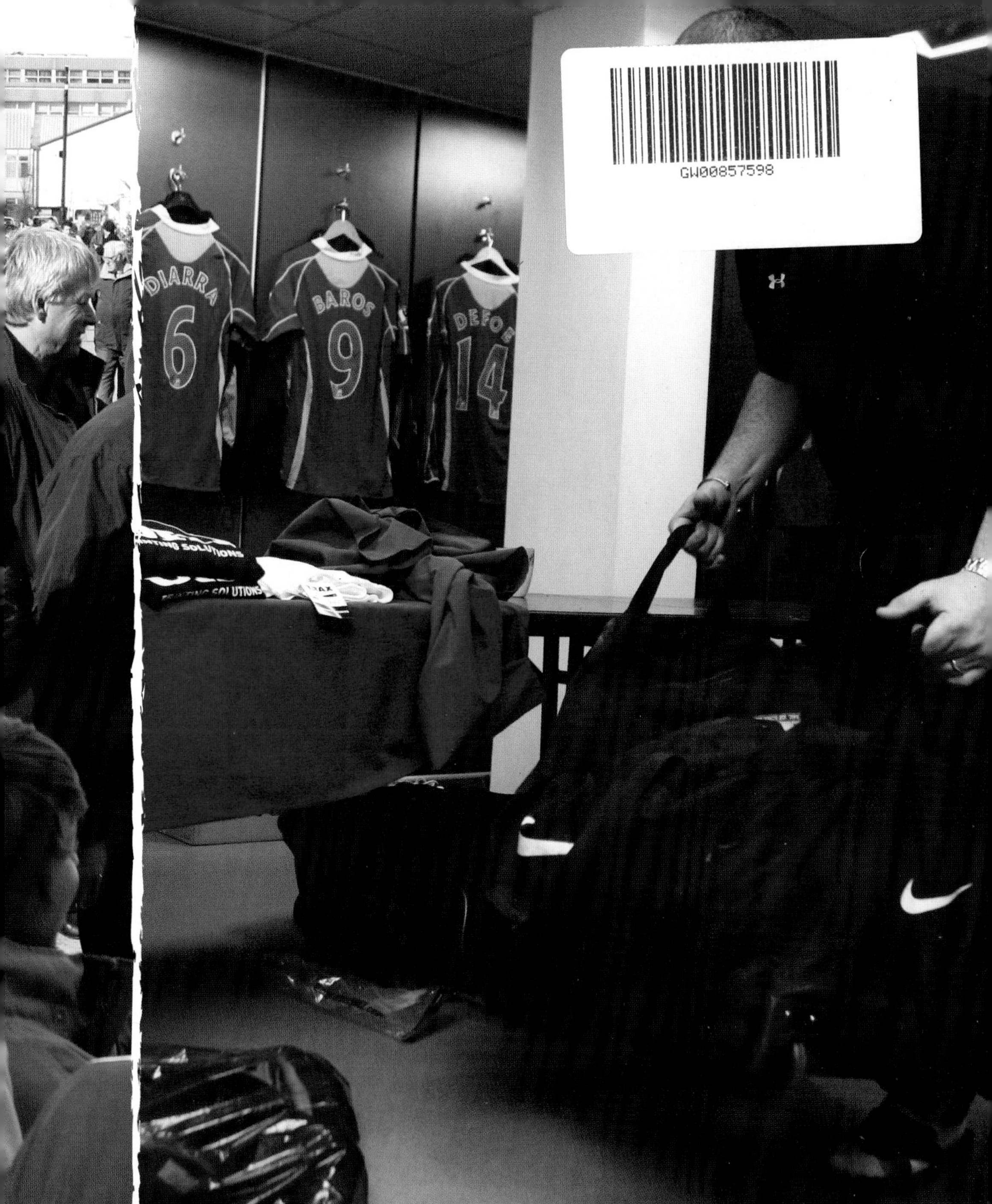

Kev is the kit man.

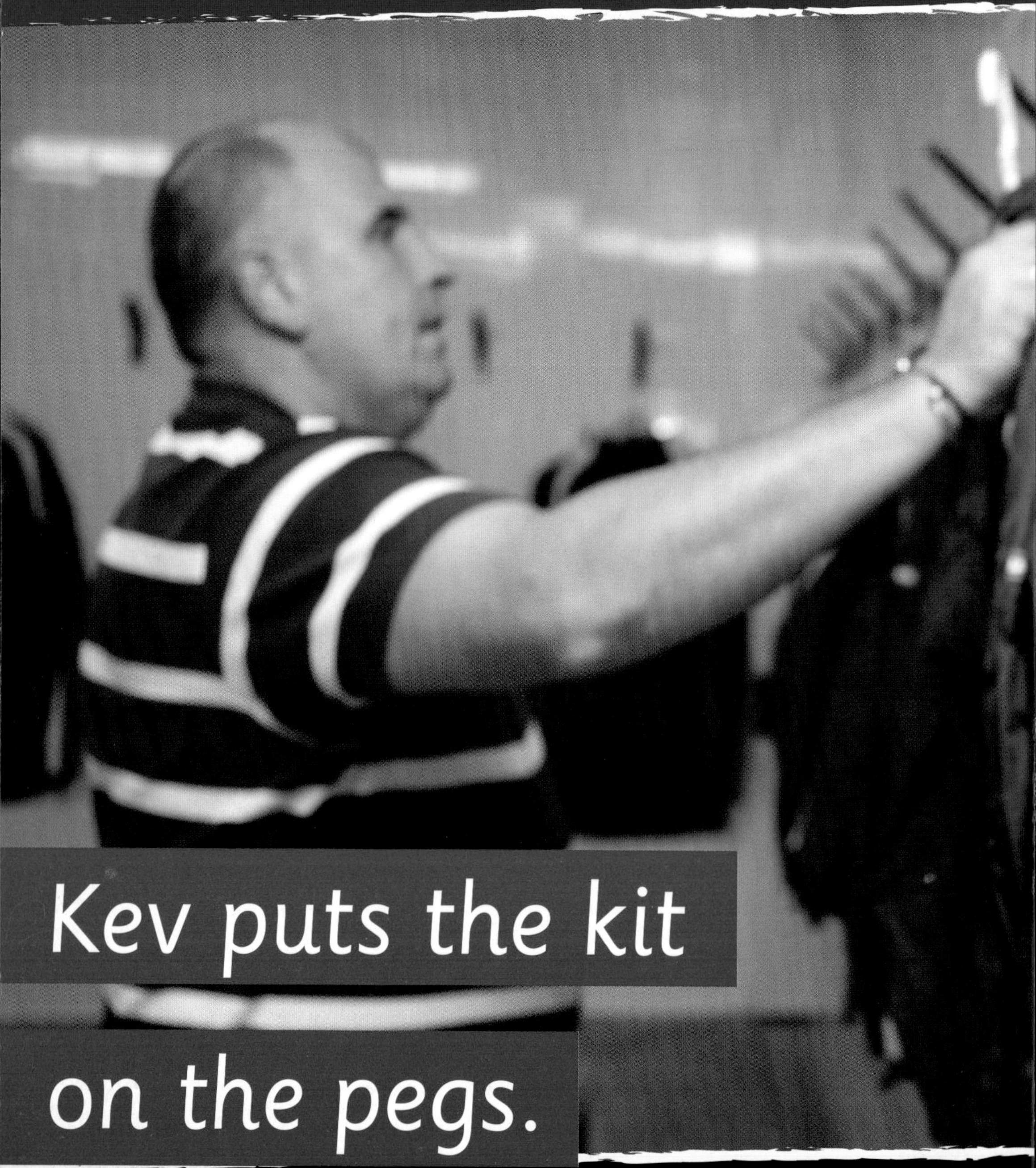

Kev puts the kit

on the pegs.

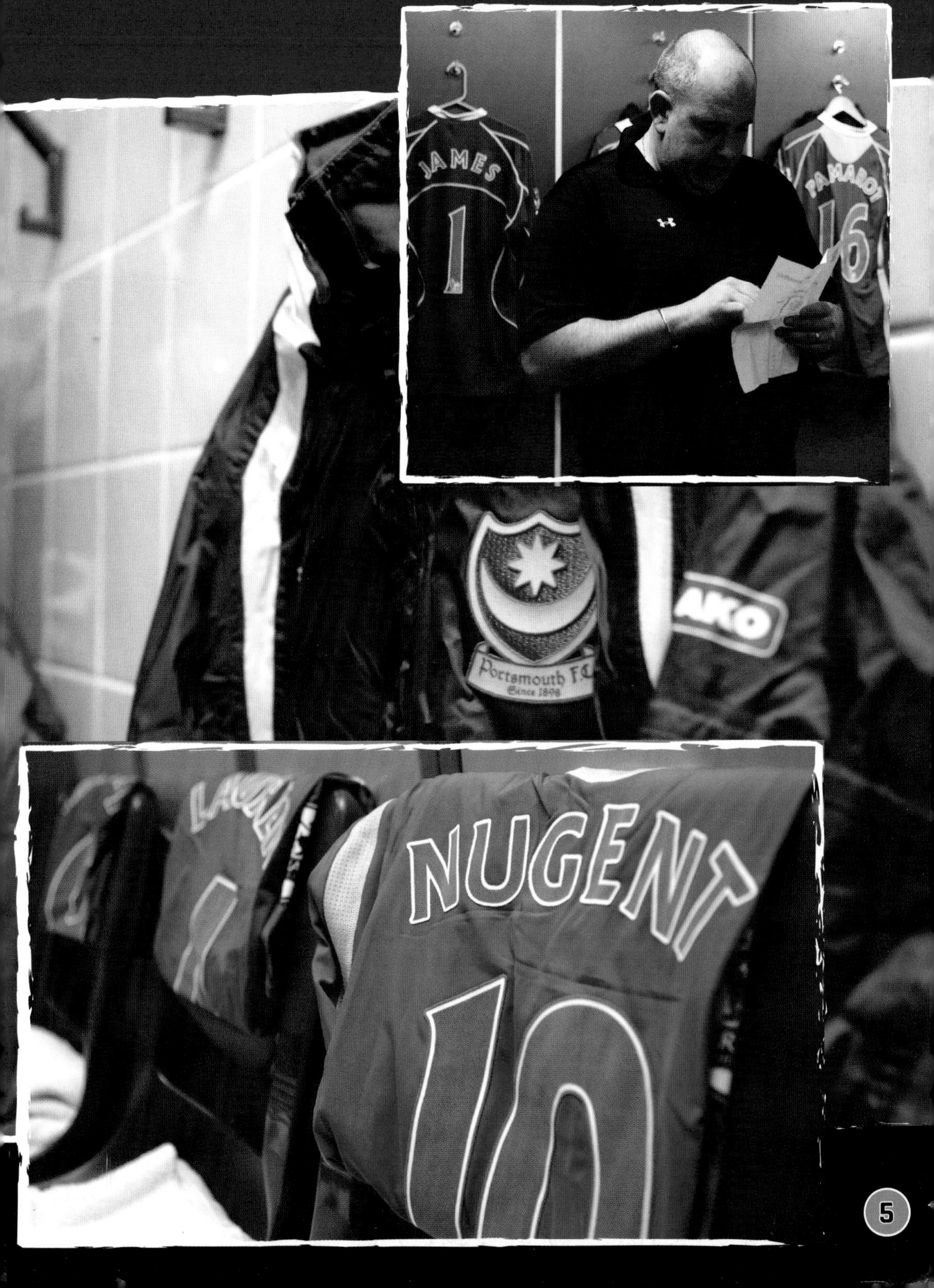
JAMES
1
Portsmouth F.C.
Since 1898
NUGENT
10

Tops, pads and boots …

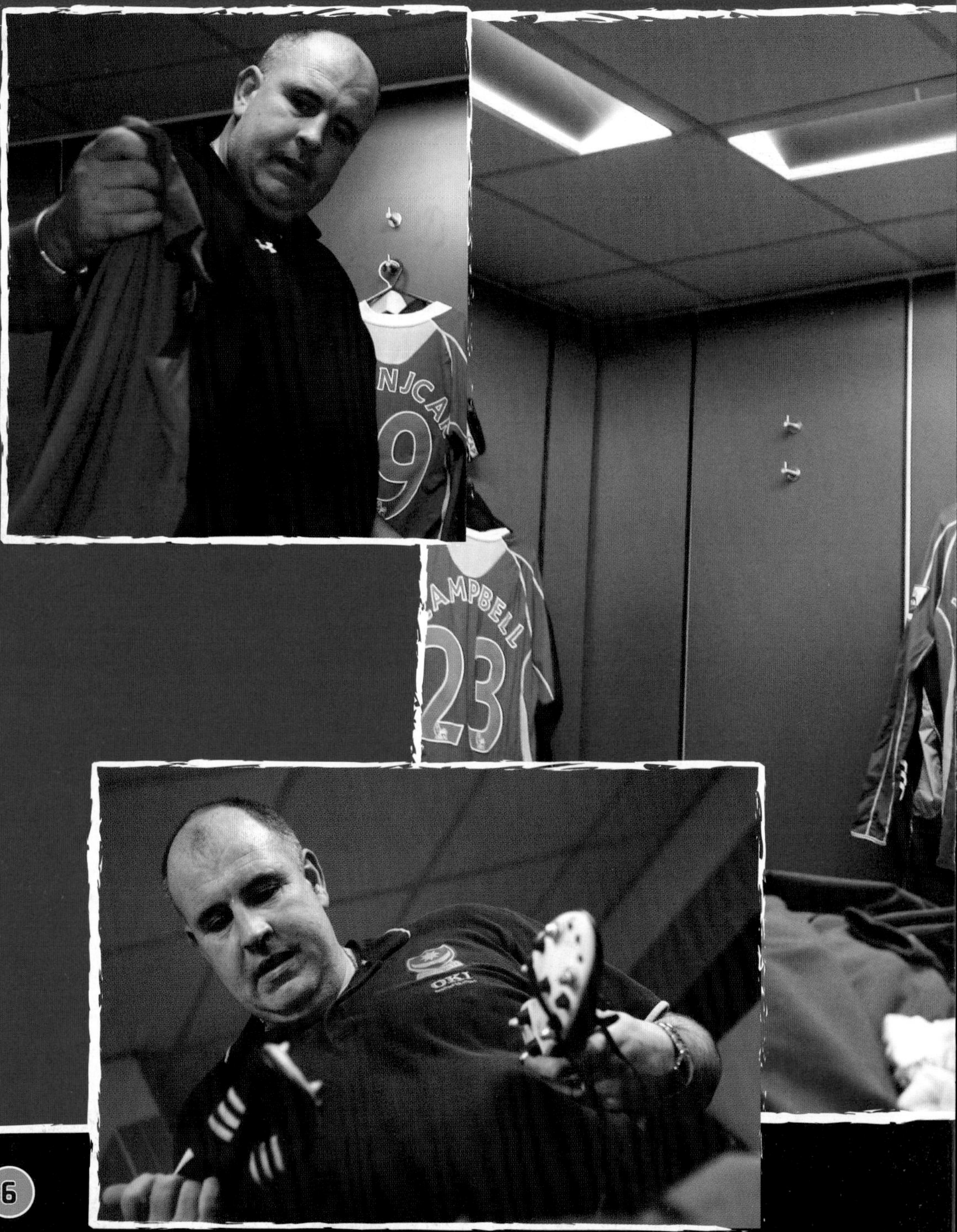

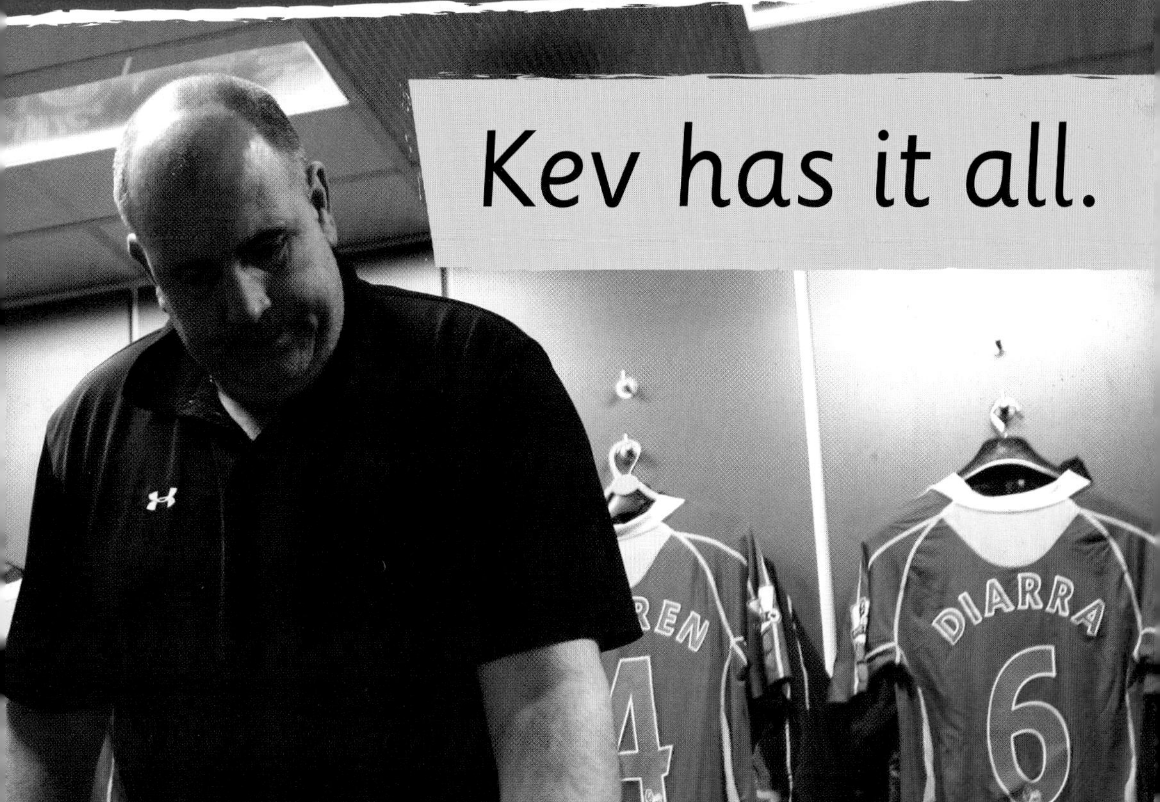

Kev has it all.

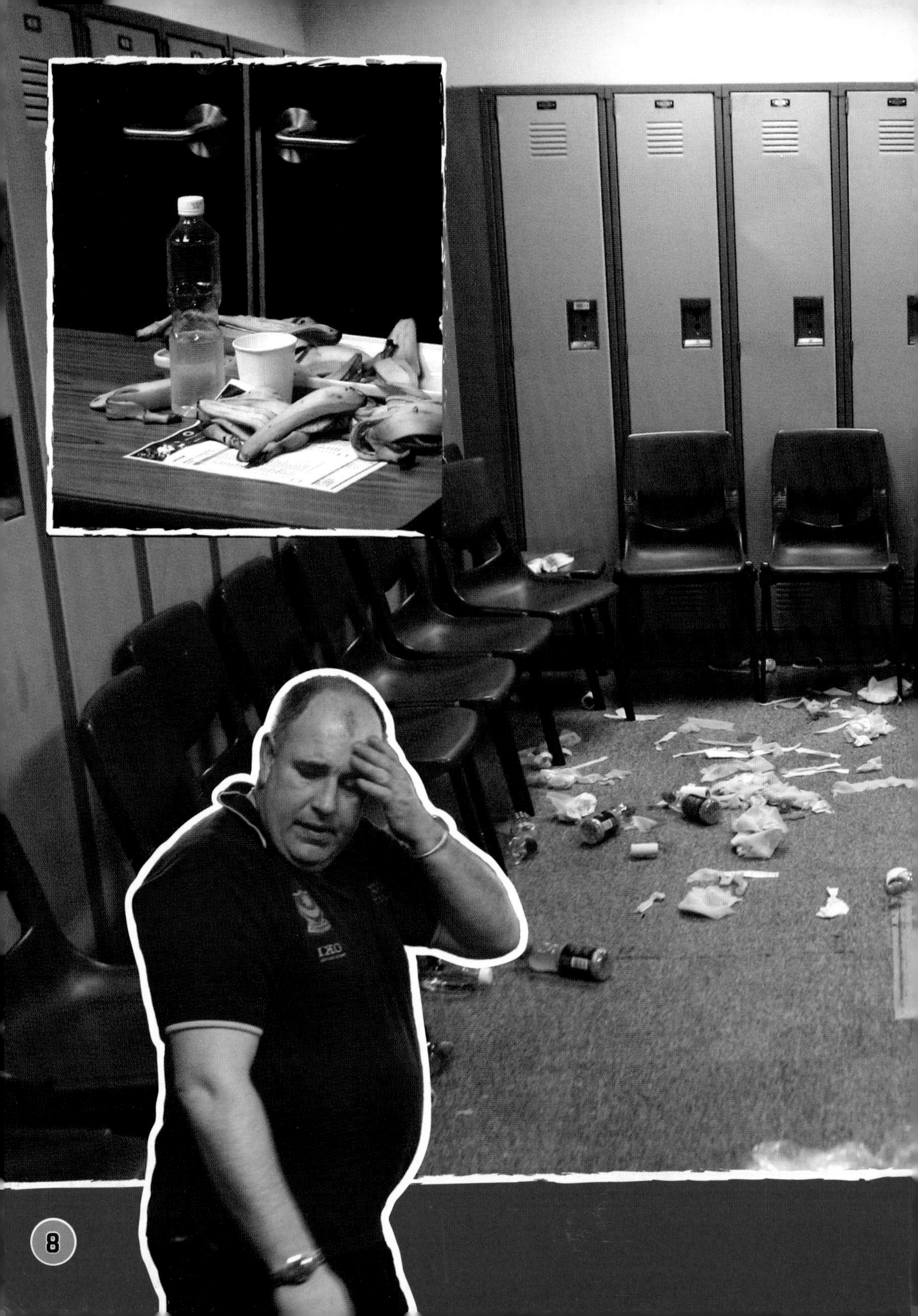

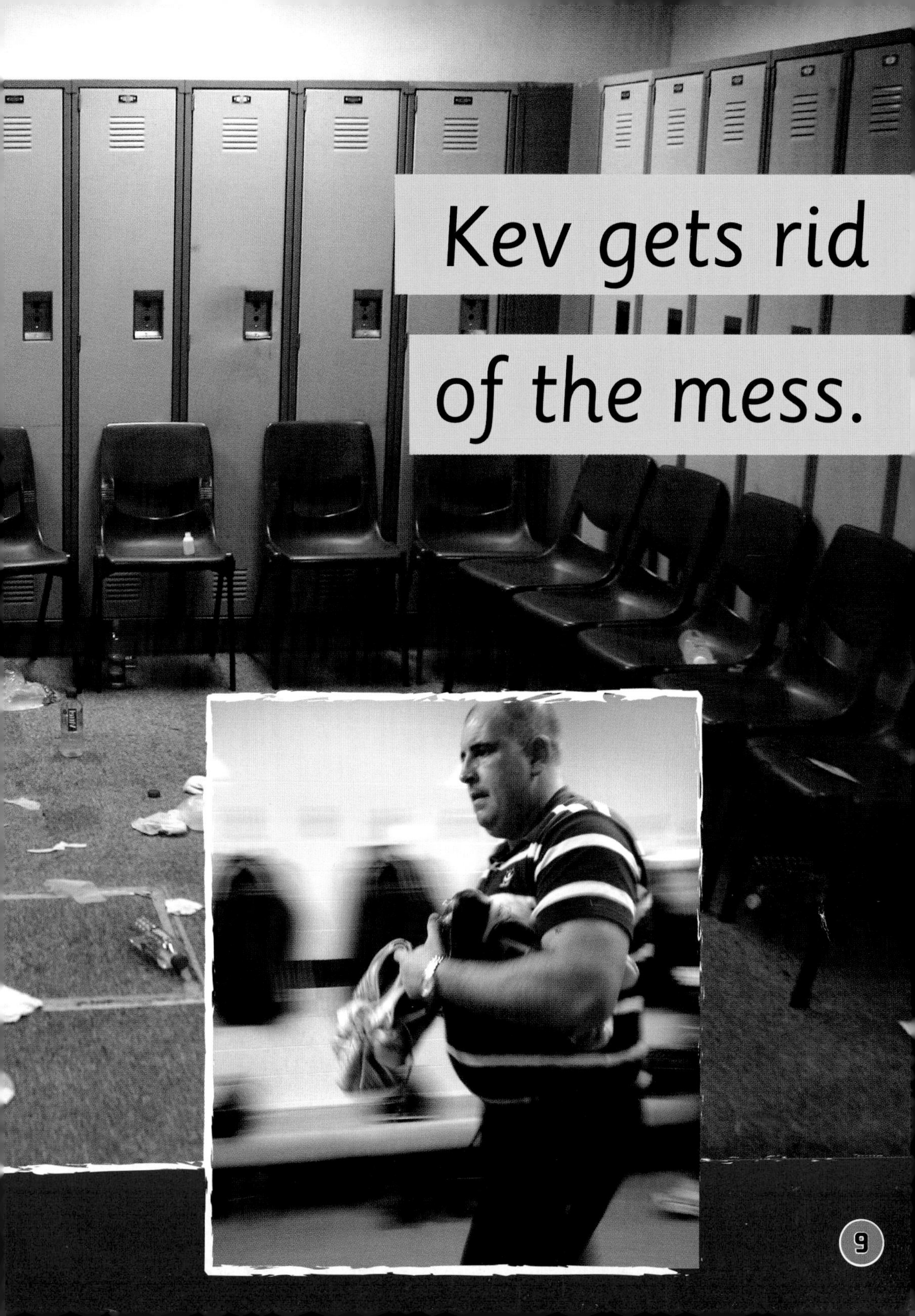

Kev gets rid of the mess.

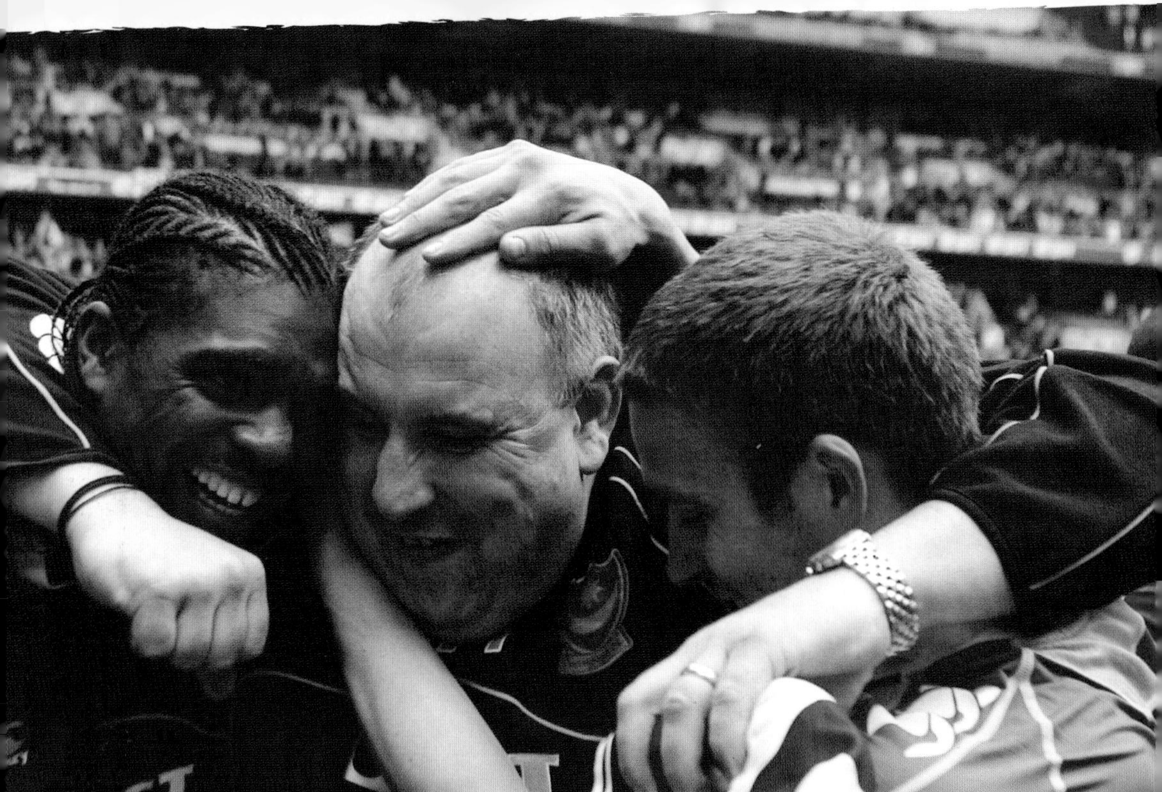

Top job, Kev!